ARTHUR'S
Mystery Babysitter

by Marc Brown

LITTLE, BROWN AND COMPANY
New York ~ Boston

Mom and Dad were getting ready to go out.

"Who's going to take care of us tonight?" asked D.W.
Dad looked at Mom. "It's a surprise," he said.

"We're used to the regular babysitters," said D.W.
"And they're used to us," Arthur added.
"We don't want a mystery babysitter!" D.W. insisted.

"All of our regular babysitters were busy," said Dad.
"We were lucky to get this one."

D.W. didn't feel lucky. "Does our mystery babysitter know about Kate?" she asked. "Some babysitters don't like babies."

"This babysitter knows all about Kate," said Dad.
"Don't worry, everything will be fine."

But Arthur and D.W. were worried.

"What if the babysitter's a pirate?" said D.W.
"A pirate wouldn't like it if we made one tiny little mistake."

"Or what if it's a robot?" D.W. went on.
"A really bossy robot that ordered us around."

"What if it's an alien from outer space?" said Arthur.
"An alien in disguise. An alien checking out Earth before a big
invasion." He gasped. "Or it could even be worse than that!"
D.W. gulped. "What could be worse than aliens from outer space?"

The doorbell rang.
"That must be the mystery babysitter now," said Mr. Read.
"Right on time. A good sign, don't you think, dear?"
Mrs. Read nodded.

Arthur and D.W. held their breath.

The door opened.
"Grandma Thora!" Arthur and D.W. shouted.
"You're the mystery babysitter?"
"Of course," she said.

D.W. jumped up and down.
"Grandma Thora, I'm so glad you're not a pirate . . .

"Thanks, kids," said Grandma Thora. "I love you, too."